*Chatham Community Library*
*Opening Day Collection*
*September 2010*

*From*
*The Friends of the Pittsboro Memorial Library*
*New Library Fund*

*Gift of*
*Pittsboro Kiwanis*

# A cab-driving thief is on the loose!

Mr. Jansen stood back. He looked at his parents and asked, "Are you hurt?"

"No," Granny said. "The cab driver just told us to get out of his cab. So we did."

"You should have seen him drive off," Gramps added. "Someone should have given him a ticket for speeding."

Granny told the police officers, "We were looking for another cab when I realized he had our luggage and the two birthday gifts we brought along. It's all in the trunk of his cab."

Gramps said, "That's why he drove off so fast. And that's why he left us far away from anyone who could help us. He didn't just want us out of his cab. He wanted to keep our luggage and gifts."

# The Cam Jansen Adventure Series

DON'T FORGET ABOUT THE YOUNG CAM JANSEN
SERIES FOR YOUNGER READERS!

# CamJansen

## The Birthday
## Mystery

**David A. Adler**
Illustrated by **Susanna Natti**

PUFFIN BOOKS

PUFFIN BOOKS

Published by the Penguin Group

Penguin Young Readers Group, 345 Hudson Street, New York, New York 10014, U.S.A.

Penguin Group (Canada), 10 Alcorn Avenue, Toronto, Ontario, Canada M4V 3B2
(a division of Pearson Penguin Canada Inc.)

Penguin Books Ltd, 80 Strand, London WC2R 0RL, England

Penguin Ireland, 25 St Stephen's Green, Dublin 2, Ireland
(a division of Penguin Books Ltd)

Penguin Group (Australia), 250 Camberwell Road, Camberwell, Victoria 3124, Australia (a
division of Pearson Australia Group Pty Ltd)

Penguin Books India Pvt Ltd, 11 Community Centre, Panchsheel Park,
New Delhi - 110 017, India

Penguin Group (NZ), Cnr Airborne and Rosedale Roads, Albany, Auckland,
New Zealand (a division of Pearson New Zealand Ltd)

Penguin Books (South Africa) (Pty) Ltd, 24 Sturdee Avenue, Rosebank,
Johannesburg 2196, South Africa

Registered Offices: Penguin Books Ltd, 80 Strand, London WC2R 0RL, England

First published in the United States of America by Viking,
a member of Penguin Putnam Books for Young Readers, 2000
Published by Puffin Books, a division of Penguin Young Readers Group, 2002, 2005

7 9 10 8 6

Text copyright © David A. Adler, 2000
Illustrations copyright © Susanna Natti, 2000
All rights reserved

THE LIBRARY OF CONGRESS HAS CATALOGED THE VIKING EDITION AS FOLLOWS:

Adler, David A.
Cam Jansen and the birthday mystery / David A. Adler ; illustrated by Susanna Natti.
p. cm.— (A Cam Jansen adventure ; 20)
Summary: When Cam's grandparents are robbed on their way to her parents' surprise
birthday party, Cam uses her photographic memory to solve the mystery.
ISBN 0-670-88877-X (hardcover)
[1. Birthdays—Fiction. 2. Grandparents—Fiction. 3. Mystery and detective stories.]
I. Natti, Susanna, ill. II. Title.
PZ7.A2615 Caabf 2000
[Fic]—dc21
99-086039

Puffin Books ISBN 0-14-240354-7

Printed in the United States of America

RL: 2.0

For my niece
Ayelet Dora Adler

# Chapter One

*Quack! Quack!*

"The ducks look hungry," Cam Jansen said to her parents. "Let's feed them."

"We didn't bring bread," Cam's mother told her.

"And it's getting late," Cam's father added. "It's almost time for dinner."

Cam looked at her watch. It was getting late, but not late enough. She had to keep her parents at the park a while longer.

Cam looked around. People were sitting

on benches. An old man and woman walked by. They were holding hands. There were ducks on the lake. A boy and his mother were riding in a small boat. "Let's walk around the lake," Cam suggested, "or rent a boat."

"No," Mr. Jansen told her. "We must get home."

Cam's parents started toward the parking lot. Cam didn't. She blinked her eyes and said, "*Click.*" Then she closed her eyes and called to her parents, "Give me a memory quiz. Ask me how many ducks are on the lake. Ask me how many people are sitting on benches."

Mr. Jansen turned and said, "OK. How many ducks are on the lake?"

Cam has a photographic memory. It's as if she has a mental camera with pictures in her head of whatever she has seen. When Cam wants to be sure to remember something, she blinks her eyes and says, "*Click.*" Cam says

"*Click*" is the sound her mental camera makes when it takes a picture.

With her eyes still closed, Cam looked at the picture she had in her head. She counted the ducks.

The boy in the boat threw a pebble into the lake.

*Quack! Quack! Quack!*

Six ducks flew off.

"There are twelve ducks," Cam said with her eyes still closed.

"I'm sorry," Cam's father told her, and smiled. "There are only six ducks swimming on the lake."

Cam opened her eyes and counted the ducks.

"I was wrong!" Cam said. "But I *clicked*! I'm never wrong when I *click*!"

"Six and six are twelve," Mr. Jansen joked. "Maybe your mental camera took a double exposure."

"Don't tease Cam," Mrs. Jansen told her

husband. Then she said to Cam, "There's nothing wrong with your camera. When you *clicked* there were twelve ducks in the lake. Some of them flew off."

Cam's real name is Jennifer, but when people found out about her amazing photographic memory, they nicknamed her "The Camera." Soon her nickname was shortened to "Cam."

Cam looked at the many people sitting on

benches. She blinked her eyes and said, "*Click.*" Then she closed her eyes.

"Now ask me about the benches," Cam said. "Ask me about the people sitting on them."

Mr. Jansen asked, "What color is the shirt of the man sitting on the bench close to the lake?"

Cam smiled. "You're trying to trick me," she answered. "There's a woman sitting on that bench. She's wearing a blue jacket, a blue-and-green striped shirt, and white pants. Her hair is red, like mine, and she's wearing a scarf."

"You're right," Mr. Jansen said. "You really do have an amazing memory. Now let's go home."

Cam opened her eyes. She looked at her watch.

"Oh, no!" Cam said. "It's so late. Let's hurry home."

As they walked to their car, Mr. Jansen said

to Cam, "At first, you wanted to stay here. Now you're in a rush to get home. You're acting funny."

"I'm just acting *hungry*," Cam told her father. "I want to go home and eat dinner."

"Maybe we should go to a restaurant," Mrs. Jansen said when they were in the car.

"Oh, no!" Cam said. "Let's eat at home. We have egg salad and spinach left from lunch. That's what I want."

Mrs. Jansen turned and looked at Cam. "At lunch you said you hated egg salad and spinach. You *are* acting funny."

They drove for a while. Then they turned the corner onto their block.

"It's Sunday," Mrs. Jansen said as they got close to their house. "Why are so many cars parked here? What's going on?"

# Chapter Two

Cam was right behind her parents as they walked from the car to the front of the house. Mr. Jansen opened the door.

*"Surprise!"*

The hall and living room were filled with friends and family. Many of them were wearing party hats. Some were blowing noise makers. There were lots of *Happy Birthday!* and *Congratulations!* signs.

Cam's parents looked around. They were both smiling.

Cam and the party guests sang, "Happy

birthday to you. Happy birthday to you. Happy birthday, Jane and Barry. Happy birthday to you."

"This is such a surprise," Mr. Jansen said.

"All our favorite people are here," Mrs. Jansen added.

Cam's friend Eric Shelton was at the party. So were his parents, with his twin sisters, Donna and Diane, and his baby brother, Howie.

"Excuse me, please. Excuse me," Mr. Shelton called out. He carried in a large cake.

The cake was covered with pink icing. *"40 and 40"* was written in blue icing in the center of the cake.

Mr. and Mrs. Jansen's fortieth birthdays were during the week, just a few days apart.

"Whose idea was this?" Mrs. Jansen asked.

"It was Cam's," Eric said. "She planned the party. She kept you at the park so we could set everything up."

Mrs. Jansen's parents were at the party. She

hugged and kissed them. She hugged her friends.

"Surprise! I'm here!" Cam's aunt Molly called out.

She hugged Mrs. Jansen and said, "I'm really surprised to be here. I travel so much that sometimes I don't know where I am."

"Molly works for an airline," Mrs. Jansen explained to the people nearby.

"Granny and Gramps are coming, too," Cam told her father.

"They should be here soon," Mr. Shelton added. "Their flight should have landed about an hour ago."

Aunt Molly said, "My flight landed this morning. I know where I am today. I'm here. But I don't remember where I was yesterday."

"I'm just happy you came to our party," Mrs. Jansen told her.

"Me, too," Cam said.

Mr. Shelton called out, "Let's eat," and everyone followed him into the dining room.

Mr. Shelton set the cake on the table. There were also plates of cookies, baby carrots, and celery sticks. There were bowls of pretzels, and popcorn, too.

Mrs. Jansen cut a slice of birthday cake and gave it to Aunt Molly. She was about to cut another slice when the phone rang.

Mr. Jansen lifted the receiver and said, "Hello."

He listened for a moment. Then he said, "Oh, my. That's terrible." He listened some

more and said, "We'll be right there. Meanwhile, you call the police."

"That was Granny. She and Gramps were robbed," Mr. Jansen said as he hurried to the door. "They're alone in the airport parking lot, and I'm going to get them."

"I'm going, too," Mrs. Jansen said.

# Chapter Three

Cam's parents hurried out of the house. Cam and Eric followed them.

Mr. and Mrs. Jansen got into the front seat of the car, closed the car doors, and drove off. They were in too much of a hurry, and too upset, to notice that Cam and Eric were in the back.

"It's our party. I was just cutting the cake when we left," Mrs. Jansen said as they turned the corner. "Maybe one of us should have stayed."

"They're our friends," Mr. Jansen said. "They understand."

"And my father is good at cutting cake," Eric said.

Cam's parents turned. They saw Cam and Eric sitting in the back.

"You shouldn't be here. You should be at the party," Cam's mother told them.

"I want to see Granny and Gramps," Cam said.

"And there's a thief to catch," Eric said.

"And maybe there's a mystery to solve," Cam added. "You know I love solving mysteries."

They were driving on a highway now. There was a large green sign ahead, pointing the way to the airport.

"We're going to the airport to pick up Granny and Gramps. Nothing else!" Cam's father said sternly. "If there's a mystery, the police will solve it."

They were at the airport now. They drove through a short tunnel under a runway. Then they drove on a winding road through the airport. On one side, people were hurrying to board planes. On the other side was a large parking lot.

"Look for them," Mr. Jansen said. "Granny said they're in section four of the parking lot."

There was a path for people walking to and from the parking lot. The light above it had turned red. Mr. Jansen stopped the car and people walked past.

16

"Look for them," Mr. Jansen said again.

There were so many people crossing in front of their car that Cam couldn't see everyone.

The traffic light changed to green. Cam, Eric, and Cam's parents kept looking for Cam's grandparents.

*Honk! Honk!*

The driver waiting behind their car wanted to go.

Mr. Jansen lowered his window. "Granny! Gramps!" he called.

The people closest to the car turned, but they weren't Cam's grandparents.

*Honk! Honk!*

"I'm parking in section four," Mr. Jansen said. He drove to the parking lot entrance.

Mr. Jansen drove to the gate. He pulled out a time card. The gate went up and he entered the lot.

"Granny! Gramps!" Mr. Jansen called as he drove slowly through the lot.

"Granny! Gramps!" Cam called.

The airport was noisy. Planes were landing nearby. Horns were honking. No one heard Mr. Jansen and Cam.

It was a very large lot. The parking spots closest to the path were taken. Mr. Jansen drove to an almost empty part of the lot. He parked against the fence.

Mr. Jansen hurried out of the car. Cam and Eric were about to follow him when Mrs. Jansen stopped them.

"Don't run ahead," she told Cam and Eric. "This airport is a big place. I don't want you to get lost."

Cam, Eric, and Mrs. Jansen started toward the path. Then Mrs. Jansen stopped.

"I'm depending on you and your photographic memory," she told Cam, "to remember where our car is parked."

Their car was parked between a small red sports car and a gray van loaded with luggage. Cam stood back so she could see the Jansens' car, the sports car, and the loaded van. She blinked her eyes and said, "*Click!*"

# Chapter Four

There were lots of people on the path. Many of them had luggage. When Cam, Eric, and Mrs. Jansen got close to the path, Eric whispered to Cam, "Let's look for the thief, too."

"That's a good idea," Cam whispered back.

A man wearing a dark suit and red bow tie rushed past. Cam looked at him, blinked her eyes and said, "*Click!*"

Cam looked at a man with long blond hair who was wearing a dark blue jacket. She blinked her eyes, and said "*Click!*"

She looked at a woman running past. The

woman had her long brown hair in a pony-
tail. Cam blinked her eyes and said, "*Click!*"
again.

Mr. Jansen was in the middle of the crowd.
"Where are they?" he asked. He was upset.
"This is section four of the parking lot, and
my parents are not here!"

*Rrrrr! Rrrrr!*

A police car entered the lot. Its lights were flashing and its siren was blaring. Mr. Jansen held up his arms. He waved wildly to the police and they drove over.

"Were you the people who called us? Were you robbed?" the policewoman driving the car asked.

"My parents were robbed," Mr. Jansen answered. "They called us and said they were in section four. But we can't find them."

"This is a very large parking lot," the policeman sitting next to the driver said. "The thief probably drove your parents to an empty part of the lot before he robbed them. That way, your parents couldn't call out to anyone and the thief could escape."

"Get in the back," the policewoman said. "We'll find them."

Cam, Eric, and Cam's parents squeezed into the backseat of the police car.

The airport had just one parking lot. The side closest to the terminals was filled with cars. Beyond that, the lot was empty. The policewoman drove to the far end of section four.

"Look over there," the policeman said.

Two people were sitting by the fence. As the police car got closer, Cam shouted, "There they are!"

"Yes," Mr. Jansen said. "Those are my parents!"

# Chapter Five

When the car stopped, Mr. Jansen hurried to his parents. Cam, Eric, Mrs. Jansen, and the police officers were right behind him.

Mr. Jansen hugged and kissed his parents.

"Hi, Granny. Hi, Gramps," Cam said. Then she and her mother hugged them, too.

Mr. Jansen stood back. He looked at his parents and asked, "Are you hurt?"

"No," Granny said. "The cab driver just told us to get out of his cab. So we did."

"You should have seen him drive off,"

Gramps added. "Someone should have given him a ticket for speeding."

Granny told the police officers, "We were looking for another cab when I realized he had our luggage and the two birthday gifts we brought along. It's all in the trunk of his cab."

Gramps said, "That's why he drove off so fast. And that's why he left us far away from anyone who could help us. He didn't just want us out of his cab. He wanted to keep our luggage and gifts."

Granny said, "When we realized we were robbed, I called you on my cell phone."

"I'm Officer Taylor," the policewoman said as she took a pen and pad from her pocket. "Can you describe the man?"

"Of course I can describe him," Granny answered. "He wasn't polite. He was greedy and not honest."

"Please," Officer Taylor said. "Tell us what he looks like."

"Is he tall or short?" the policeman asked. "Is he fat or thin? What color are his eyes? His hair? What is he wearing?"

Cam's grandparents looked at each other. They thought for a moment.

"We never saw his face," Granny said. "He sat in the front seat of the cab and he never turned to look at us."

Officer Taylor asked, "Can you describe the cab?"

"It was yellow," Gramps said, "and there were candy wrappers on the floor."

Officer Taylor closed her pad and put it back in her pocket.

"There are hundreds of cabs here," she said. "They're all yellow and probably all have candy wrappers on the floor. Without a better description, we can't help you."

"You mean all our things are gone?" Gramps asked. "You mean the gifts are gone? That's why he robbed us. He saw those gift-wrapped boxes and he wanted them."

The policeman smiled. "I'm Officer Mill-veckstein," he said to Cam's grandparents. "Most people call me Officer M. Just think for a moment. I'm sure you really did see the driver."

Officer M took out his pad and waited.

"Well," Granny said. "I saw the back of his head, and he has long blond hair."

"He's wearing a black jacket," Gramps added. "There was a really big dent in the side of his cab. I remember that because it was hard to open the door."

28

"Now that's something," Officer M said. "We'll go to the terminal, where the cabs wait. Maybe we'll find the thief there, or maybe one of the other cab drivers will be able to help us."

"I'm sorry," Officer M told Cam, Eric, and Cam's parents, "but we don't have room for all of you in our car."

Cam's grandparents got into the back of the police car. The car drove off. Cam, Eric, and Cam's parents started to walk toward the terminal.

"I may have seen him," Cam whispered to Eric. "I may have seen the thief." Then Cam closed her eyes and said, "*Click!*"

# Chapter Six

"When we got out of our car, I saw a man with long blond hair and a dark blue jacket. In the cab, Granny and Gramps may have thought the jacket was black," Cam whispered to Eric with her eyes still closed. "He was on the path walking toward the terminal."

Cam's parents were walking ahead of her and Eric. Mr. Jansen turned and said, "We'll go back to the car. We'll wait there for Granny and Gramps."

Cam opened her eyes.

"But I want to be with Granny and Gramps," Cam said. "Maybe we can help them catch the thief."

Mr. Jansen told Cam, "Catching a thief may be dangerous. It's a job for the police."

"But I think I saw him," Cam said.

She told her parents about the man on the path.

"Cam has to tell the police what she saw," Mrs. Jansen said. "And then, instead of sitting in the car, we can wait in the terminal, on those comfortable chairs."

It was a long walk across the parking lot. Cam *clicked* again and looked at the picture she had in her head of the man in the dark blue jacket.

"He's wearing a red scarf, sunglasses, and boots," Cam said, "and he was walking very fast."

They were walking on the path now, with lots of other people who were on their way to the terminal. Many of them were carrying luggage. None of them was wearing a dark blue or black jacket.

At the end of the path was a traffic light and a *Walk—Don't Walk* sign. People stopped there and waited for the *Walk* sign to light up.

People were waiting across the road, too. They were on their way to the parking lot. Many of them were also carrying luggage.

Cam watched cabs ride past and let their passengers off at the curb. Then the cabs joined the end of the line waiting to take people from the airport.

The *Walk* sign lit up. The path across the road was quickly crowded with people walking to and from the terminal.

"There they are," Eric called out. He pointed to Cam's grandparents and the two police officers. They were looking at the long line of cabs waiting by the curb.

Cam ran to them. She told Officer M about the man in the dark blue jacket.

"If he's the thief, why would he be walking in the parking lot?" Officer M asked.

Cam was thinking about that when her parents and Eric caught up with her.

"Did you tell them who you saw?" Cam's mother asked.

"Yes," Cam answered, "but now I'm not sure he's the thief."

Just then Officer Taylor pointed to a cab

that had just stopped by the curb. There was
a large dent in its side. Two people got out of
the cab.

"Is that the cab you were in?" she asked
Cam's grandparents.

They turned to look at it.

Gramps said, "It's hard to tell from here."

"Let's go," Officer Taylor said. "Let's take a closer look."

The cab started to drive off.

"Hey! Stop!" Officer Taylor shouted.

She and Officer M ran to the middle of the street and held up their hands.

Granny and Gramps ran after them. Cam and Eric started to run, too.

"Wait here," Cam's father told Cam and Eric. "The police don't need your help."

*Screech!*

The cab quickly stopped.

Officer M poked his head into the window of the cab. Then the door on the driver's side began to open.

"They've caught him," Eric declared. "They've caught the thief!"

# Chapter Seven

The driver got out of the cab. He was bald and he was wearing a blue sweater.

"Where's his blond hair and black jacket?" Mr. Jansen asked.

"Maybe he was wearing a blond wig when he stole the luggage," Eric said. "And maybe he took off his jacket."

The cab driver spoke to the police and Cam's grandparents for a while. He opened the trunk of his cab. It was empty. The police thanked him. The driver got back in his car and drove off.

"Hey," Eric said and pointed to a cab at the end of the line. It had a large dent in its hood. "The thief may be in one of the other smashed cars."

Cam looked at the cab with the dented hood. Then she saw another cab stop. A man got out. He was carrying a small suitcase. Cam looked at the front of the line. A woman and a small child got into a cab while the driver loaded two large suitcases into the trunk.

Cam's grandparents and the two police officers returned to the curb. Eric and Cam's parents watched them look at each of the cabs.

Cam didn't. She closed her eyes and said, "*Click!*"

As a cab at the front of the line drove off, all the others moved up. Others kept joining the end of the line.

Cam said, "*Click!*" again.

"There's one with a large dent on the side," Eric said and pointed to the end of the line.

Cam opened her eyes. "I just remembered something," she said. "Let's go to our car."

"No," Eric told her. "I think I found the cab. I am going to tell the police officers. I want to watch them catch the thief."

The police looked into a cab in the middle of the line. Then the door opened and the driver got out. The driver was a woman with long blond hair. She was wearing a blue denim jacket.

Eric said, "I'm going to show them the cab with the dent."

Mrs. Jansen said, "I'll go with you."

"I'll be waiting for you in our car," Cam told Eric and Mrs. Jansen as they walked off.

"Maybe looking in cabs is not the best way to catch the thief," Cam told her father. "Maybe there's a better way."

"What are you saying?" he asked.

"I'm saying, I think I know how to catch the thief. I know how to get back Granny and Gramps's luggage and the birthday gifts. I just need to go to our car and look at something."

"Then let's go," Mr. Jansen said.

Cam and Mr. Jansen walked quickly toward the parking lot. The *Don't Walk* sign was lit. Cam and her father stopped and waited for it to change.

"Look at the people on both sides of the road," Cam said. "Lots of them are carrying luggage."

"So what?" Cam's father asked.

The *Walk* sign lit up. Cam and her father crossed the road to the parking lot.

"So what?" Cam's father asked again.

"I'll show you," Cam said. She led him to the almost empty part of the lot where their car was parked. The red sports car and the gray van on either side of the Jansens' car were still there. Cam looked through the back windows of the van. Then she told her father to look, too.

"What do you see?" Cam asked.

"Suitcases," Mr. Jansen answered. "So what? Lots of people bring suitcases to an airport."

"That's right," Cam said. "But they don't leave them in their cars. They either park here and take their luggage onto an airplane. Or they get off an airplane, bring their luggage to their cars, and leave the parking lot."

Mr. Jansen looked at his daughter and smiled. "You're right," he said. "Why would a van be parked here loaded with luggage?"

"Mom told me to remember where our car was parked," Cam said. "That's why I looked at our car, the sports car, and the van, and *clicked!* That's why I remembered the luggage in the back of the van."

Mr. Jansen looked through the back windows of the van again. "And there are two large gift-wrapped boxes in there," he said. "I'll bet those are our birthday gifts. We have to show this to the police."

"I'm not leaving here," Cam said. "The thief might come back with more stolen luggage. He might load it in the van and drive off."

Cam's father asked, "What would he do with the cab?"

"Maybe the cab is stolen. Maybe he'll just leave it here," Cam answered.

Mr. Jansen looked at the luggage in the back of the van. Then he told Cam, "You're not staying here alone. We'll wait in the car and see what happens. But we're not chasing any thief."

# Chapter Eight

Cam and her father got in their car. Cam was in the back. Her father was in the front. They locked the doors.

They watched cars ride along the road, just on the other side of the parking lot fence. Each time they saw a cab, Cam and her father wondered if the thief was driving it.

Mr. Jansen pointed to the gray van and said, "That may not be the thief's."

Cam said, "I think it is."

"Well, maybe it's not," Mr. Jansen said. "Maybe someone got here early for his flight.

It was too early to bring his luggage to the terminal, so he's eating dinner in one of the restaurants. Or maybe he's buying a ticket now to go somewhere."

"Look!" Cam whispered.

A cab was going by the fence very slowly. Cam looked at the cab. She blinked her eyes and said, "*Click!*"

Cam and her father watched the cab turn into the parking lot entrance. It was in the middle of the lot, a long way from the van and the Jansens' car. The cab turned.

"Did you see the big dent in the door?" Cam asked.

"I saw it," Mr. Jansen whispered. "And I see what he's doing. He's checking that there's no one here."

The cab turned again. Now it was coming back toward the van and much closer than the first time.

"Get down!" Mr. Jansen said. "Don't let him see us."

Cam and her father fell to the floor. They waited and listened.

Cam heard a car door open. Then she heard other car noises.

Cam slowly moved up until she could peek out the window.

The cab was right by the van. Its door and trunk were open. A man with blond hair, wearing a black leather jacket, was loading a suitcase into the van.

Cam dropped to the floor again and listened. She heard an engine start. She waited. Then she peeked out. The van was still there. The cab was driving off.

Cam told her father, "He's gone."

Mr. Jansen peeked out the window.

Cam said, "He's probably going to steal someone else's luggage."

The cab went just a short way off. Then it stopped right by the fence. The driver got out and walked toward the van.

Mr. Jansen dropped to the floor again. Cam did, too.

"This is it," Mr. Jansen whispered. "He's finished his dirty business for the day. He's leaving the cab here. He's going to drive off with the luggage and our birthday gifts."

Cam said, "We can't let him get away. We have to stop him."

They heard the van door open.

Mr. Jansen said, "We're not trained to stop criminals. That's a job for the police."

They heard the van engine start.

Cam said, "Before he can leave the lot, he has to pay for parking here like everyone else. Let's get ahead of him. When it's time to pay, you can tell the man in the booth to call the police."

Mr. Jansen sat up. "That's a great idea," he said. "We'll keep our doors locked and I'll just be someone in a hurry to leave the parking lot."

The van was already on its way to the exit. Mr. Jansen quickly started his car. He sped in front of the van.

*Honk! Honk!*

The thief tried to pass, but Mr. Jansen wouldn't let him.

*Honk! Honk!*

They were near the exit now. Mr. Jansen got in line, just in front of the thief.

"That was scary," Mr. Jansen said. "I sure hope he doesn't know we think he's the thief. I hope he doesn't drive to the other exit."

"There's another exit?" Cam asked.

Mr. Jansen nodded. "It's on the other side of the lot."

The gate went up. The car ahead drove off. Now it was Mr. Jansen's turn to pay.

"Ticket please," the man in the booth said.

Mr. Jansen whispered, "You have to call the police. The man behind us is a thief."

"Ticket please," the man in the booth said again.

"He didn't hear you," Cam said.

Mr. Jansen wrote CALL POLICE! on his ticket. THE MAN BEHIND US IS A THIEF! He handed the ticket to the man in the booth.

The man looked at the ticket. He looked at Mr. Jansen. Then he looked at the man in the van.

Cam and her father turned and looked at him, too.

The man in the booth picked up his telephone. He pressed a few buttons and then said, "This is Gary in the south parking lot

exit. Get me security. Get me the police."

The thief saw Gary talking on the telephone. He started to back up. There was a large white car right behind him.

*Honk! Honk!*

The thief honked his horn as he backed his van up. He bumped into the white car, turned, and drove off.

"He's getting away!" Cam shouted. "He's getting away!"

# Chapter Nine

A police car entered the lot. Officer Taylor was driving. Officer M, Eric, and Cam's mother and grandparents were in the police car, too.

Cam opened her window. She pointed to the gray van speeding across the lot and shouted, "Get him! He's the thief. Get him!"

The police car turned and followed the van.

*Rrrr! Rrrr!*

The police car's lights were flashing. Its

siren was blaring. It sped in front of the gray van and forced it to stop.

Mr. Jansen turned and drove to where the police car and van had stopped. Everyone was standing by the van. Its back doors were open.

"That's all my stuff," the driver told the police. "I always take a lot of clothes along when I travel."

Granny took a blue suitcase out of the van. She opened it and took out a dress and a pair of women's shoes. "Are these yours?" she asked the driver of the van.

He didn't answer.

The police arrested the driver of the van.

Officer M put Gramps and Granny's things in the trunk of the Jansen car. Granny and Gramps thanked the police officers.

"And we thank you," Officer M told Cam. "Your friend Eric said we should find out why you were waiting in the parking lot. He said you solve mysteries, and he was right."

Cam said, "I remembered there was a van parked next to our car and it was loaded with suitcases. When I saw all the people carrying their luggage to and from the terminal, I realized it was strange for someone to park here and not take his things."

"Cam has a photographic memory," Eric said. "That's why she remembered the van."

Officer Taylor thanked Cam. She locked the thief in the back of the police car and drove off. Officer M got in the van and followed them.

Cam, Eric, and Cam's parents and grandparents watched the police car and the van leave the parking lot.

"Well," Gramps said. "We have a party to go to."

"It's a surprise party for us," Mrs. Jansen said, "and the surprise is, we're not there."

They all crowded into the car and hurried home. On the way, Mr. Jansen smiled and said to Cam, "When we were driving to the airport, I told you we were not coming here to solve a mystery."

"Well, I'm glad she did," Granny said.

"Cam is always solving mysteries," Eric told Cam's grandparents.

When they arrived at the party, everyone was happy that Cam's grandparents were safe.

They sang "Happy Birthday" to Cam's parents again.

"Open our gifts," Gramps said to Mr. and Mrs. Jansen. "Take a look at what we gave you."

Mrs. Jansen unwrapped her gift. It was a video camera. Mr. Jansen's gift was a still-picture camera.

"There's film in both cameras," Gramps said. "That's part of the gift."

"Smile," Mr. Jansen told everyone.

He looked through the viewfinder of his new camera. He pressed the shutter button and the camera went, *Click!*

"Keep smiling," Cam told everyone. "My mental camera has film, too." Then Cam looked at all the happy people at the surprise birthday party. Cam blinked her eyes and said, "*Click!*"